P9-EKR-572

NAKED
VILLAINY

NAKED VILLAINY

Sara Woods

St. Martin's Press
New York

Any work of fiction whose characters were of uniform excellence could rightly be condemned – by that fact if by no other – as being incredibly dull. Therefore no excuse can be considered necessary for the villainy or folly of people appearing in this book. It seems extremely unlikely that any one of them should resemble a real person, alive or dead. Any such resemblance is completely unintentional and without malice.

S.W.

Library of Congress Cataloging in Publication Data

Woods, Sara, pseud.
  Naked villainy.

  I. Title.
PR6073.063N3 1987   823'.914   86-27925
ISBN 0-312-00163-0

First published in Great Britain by Macmillan London Limited.

First U.S. Edition

10 9 8 7 6 5 4 3 2 1

'And thus I clothe my naked villainy with odd
ends stol'n forth of holy writ and seem a
saint when most I play the devil.'
—*Richard III*, Act I, Scene *i*

Prologue

'By every rule in the book,' said Kevin O'Brien, sitting back comfortably in the wing chair that was generally reserved for Sir Nicholas Harding's use when he and his wife visited the Maitlands, 'you should be dining with me, the pair of you, which you'll remember was my first suggestion.' He sipped appreciatively the cognac, which was also kept for Sir Nicholas's delectation, and added with a smile in his hostess's direction, 'But you wouldn't be expecting me to turn down a meal of Jenny's cooking, would you now?'

They were gathered, the three of them, Jenny and Antony Maitland and their visitor, in the big, rather shabby, comfortable living room of the flat that had been contrived for the Maitlands' occupation (in the days when housing had been in very short supply) at the top of Sir Nicholas's house in Kempenfeldt Square. Jenny had taken her favourite place, curled up in one corner of the sofa, and looked quite as relaxed as O'Brien did. As for Antony, he too had taken up his favourite position, standing on the hearth-rug a little to one side of the fire, but in spite of the good talk they had enjoyed before and during dinner he wasn't quite ready to take Kevin's casual air at face value. 'You said you had something you wanted to talk to me about,' he said. 'It seemed more appropriate to do so here than at a restaurant.'

'It isn't a professional matter,' said O'Brien hastily. He was a tall, narrow-shouldered man and in repose his face had a look of austerity which disappeared as soon as he smiled. Even conversing quietly as they had been doing there was a richness about his voice, and Antony knew from experience that in court he could be very impressive indeed. 'And this time, Jenny me darlin', I can promise you won't be bored.' He was inclined to adopt the hint of a brogue on occasion, without any excuse at all, as he had been born and brought up in Yorkshire. There had been a time when Antony found this exasperating, but he knew his fellow barrister better now, as well as anyone could expect to know so enigmatic a man.

'I'm never bored,' said Jenny, which was true enough. She was a better listener than a talker, and was so used to legal shop by now that she would have missed it if none had been available.

'I came to you,' said O'Brien impressively, turning back to Maitland again, 'because you're the one man I can trust to realise the seriousness of the matter, and not to laugh your head off when I tell you either.'

'Not a professional matter,' repeated Maitland in a questioning tone. He retrieved his glass from the mantelshelf and went to sit in the chair opposite O'Brien. 'Your narrative begins to interest me, strangely,' he said.

Kevin took a quick look from one of his companions to the other. 'It's something a friend of my father's told me,' he said. 'It was in confidence, of course, but when I said I'd like a second opinion he told me he'd no objection to my passing the story on as long as I could rely on the discretion of the person or persons concerned.'

'You said—' Maitland began.

'You'll see what I mean in a moment,' Kevin promised. 'It's advice the poor man needs and there's no one he could get it from but a lawyer, but he's not in any trouble himself, nothing like that.'

Jenny, who had been watching her husband's face, turned now to observe their guest. Meeting her look, O'Brien gave her his most persuasive smile. It was obvious now to Antony that she had sensed his own uneasiness, and he took a moment, while she herself surveyed O'Brien seriously, to let his gaze linger on her. Jenny had brown-gold hair that curled closely about her head, so that she had long since given up trying to persuade it into some fashionable style. She had a short, straight nose and rather wide-set grey eyes that gave her a look of candour that he knew only too well could be used – and often was – with deliberate intent to deceive. Now she returned Kevin's smile. 'If you want Antony's advice,' she told him, 'you'll have·to explain to him what it's about.'

'And haven't I been trying to for the last ten minutes?' said O'Brien unfairly. 'My father's friend is a Frenchman, over here visiting his sister. The thing that's worrying him is that he thinks they're saying the Black Mass in the wine cellar.'

Antony had just raised his glass, and this bald statement caused him to choke over the contents. 'That isn't fair,' he protested as soon as he could speak. 'You've more or less put me on my honour not to laugh at you, and the Black Mass is bad enough and not at all amusing . . . but in the wine cellar! That's altogether too much.'

'When you think about it, even that isn't funny,' said O'Brien reprovingly.

'Not a bit,' Maitland agreed, composing himself. 'But . . . no, look here, Kevin, you can't spring a thing like this on us without warning. What's the man's name, and is he in his right mind, and who are the other people concerned?'

'All in good time. The man who consulted me is Georges Letendre, and though it's quite true he was originally a friend of my father he comes somewhere between us in age and I've more or less inherited him.'

'Letendre?' said Jenny. 'Doesn't that mean something to me?'

'It probably does,' Kevin agreed. 'Cosmetics . . . perfume—'

'Yes, of course, you see them everywhere, but I never thought of it being a person's name, just one invented for the brand.'

'It's his name all right. Georges's father started the firm. I think it's quite big business nowadays. His son, Emile, runs the English operation, but as he only has a small studio flat Georges is staying with his sister, Mrs Johnson.'

'That doesn't answer all my questions,' Antony objected.

'You asked me if he was mad; anything but. As for the other people concerned, I can't be very helpful. There's Georges's sister, Françoise, of course, and her husband, Alan Johnson. Georges mentioned a number of other names of people who were frequent visitors to their house but I can't say I remember

7

any of them except for Luke Granville, who is the Johnsons' solicitor and apparently a great friend, and his daughter, Jane, whom Emile Letendre wants to marry, but Georges – in a rather typical fit of drama – has threatened to cast him off entirely if he does.'

'Why?' asked Jenny, inclined to be indignant.

'Because he thinks she may be mixed up in this black magic business through her father's connection with the Johnsons. I don't know whether that's true or not, and I can quite understand you both being curious, but it really doesn't concern us.'

'I suppose you're coming to that,' said Maitland. 'What exactly is your problem?'

'What Georges can do about it. He thought I might have some suggestions.'

'Tell me first what gave rise to these suspicions?'

'The Letendres are Catholic, and in their family at least the usual order seems to be reversed. By which I mean that it's the male members who seem to take their religion more seriously. Georges says Françoise has had a tendency to superstition since she was a girl—'

'How old is she now?'

'Younger than he is, though I don't suppose that she can be much under fifty. But she certainly looks younger, a very beautiful woman.'

'I see. Go on, you were telling us that she was superstitious.'

'Nothing very dreadful at the time Georges is referring to. She always said it was just a bit of fun – he used the word *rigoler* but I think that is what he meant – and professed not to believe in it at all. But he also suspects she attended a seance sometimes, though when he tackled her about it she always denied it.'

'We're still a long way from the Black Mass.'

'Yes. You must understand that since her marriage he hasn't seen a great deal of her. And don't ask me how long ago that took place, because I don't know exactly; but it was certainly quite a time. I think mainly they met when she and her husband visited him in Paris, but since Emile has been living in London Georges has been over rather more frequently. Alan Johnson, I should have told you, is a historian and writer, and when he shuts himself in his study it's an understood thing that he mustn't be disturbed. So one evening when guests were expected Françoise got the key from her husband and asked her brother to go down to the cellar and select the wine for dinner. It's an enormous place – I'm quoting Georges, you know, this is all hearsay – and the wine racks are the first things you come to at the bottom of the stairs. Beyond that, there's a vast empty space, the cellar runs right under the house, no dividing walls but pillars here and there for support. But what aroused Georges's curiosity was the fact that there was none of the usual clutter that accumulates in such places, and it all looked extraordinarily clean. So when he'd selected the wine he stood it at the foot of the cellar steps and walked across to have a look at the other end. There was what I believe is called a pentacle painted on the floor, a pentagram, a five-pointed star.'

'I don't know much about witchcraft,' said Maitland slowly, 'but that certainly seems to suggest that something of the sort was going on. That would be bad enough, if true, but we're still a long way from the final blasphemy of the Black Mass.'

'I'm trying to tell this in order if only you'll listen, oh most doubting of Thomases,' said O'Brien rather impatiently. 'Still, I suppose I should be grateful that you appreciate the seriousness of the situation. There was a table there, just a bare board with nothing to show its use. And a cupboard that was locked. But there was a piece of paper jammed in the door, and though that fitted too tightly for it to be pulled out, Georges was able to tear a scrap off it. He wouldn't let me keep it but I copied down what it said. It doesn't mean a thing to me, but it's unpleasantly suggestive.'

Maitland took the scrap of paper and read: '*By Adonai, by Prerai, by Tetragrammaton, by Anexhexeton.*'

'It sounds like a – a conjuration of some kind,' he said when the words broke off. 'Do you want to look at it, Jenny love? It won't make you much wiser either.'

'It doesn't,' Jenny agreed a moment later. 'I suppose you're thinking, Kevin, that the vestments and all the things they needed were in that cupboard. But the Black Mass, that's devil worship, isn't it? A service that's a complete reversal of Christian liturgy.'

'I know it's distressing but that's why I came to Antony for

9

advice,' said Kevin, very much as he had done before. 'Because I knew you two would understand the frightfulness of it, and not just brush it off as something that doesn't matter. And as for the proof for which you are waiting so impatiently,' he added, turning to Maitland again, 'I haven't seen it, but Georges assures me it exists. A photograph of his sister lying naked upon the very table he had seen in the cellar. There were candles round about and a figure with black vestments standing behind with its arms upraised, in what was obviously the supreme moment of the ceremony.'

'You haven't seen this yourself?' Maitland insisted.

'I told you I hadn't. Georges described it for me. But if it were a picture of your sister in similar circumstances would you show it to anyone else?'

'If I had a sister, no I shouldn't. How did Monsieur Letendre come across this incriminating photograph?'

'He had some papers in the top drawer of the tallboy in his room, and one of them slipped down the back. So he had to pull the drawer all the way out, and the snapshot was there as well. Obviously one of the people in attendance had been staying in the house, and had been given it as a sort of gruesome memento. The thing is, Antony, Georges is as horrified as we are, but what can he do about it?'

'Has he confronted his sister with the snapshot?'

'He didn't think it would do any good. She'd only have laughed and said it was a sort of charade, they weren't doing anybody any harm ... except – heaven help them! – themselves.'

'Even if he wanted to inform on her, which I suppose he doesn't,' said Maitland slowly, 'it presents rather a problem. The Witchcraft Act of 1736 was repealed when the Fraudulent Mediums Act came into force ... I remember all that because of that case of Uncle Nick's a few years ago. I expect you've looked up blasphemy—'

'It's an offence at common law punishable by a fine or imprisonment,' said O'Brien promptly.

'Yes, but nobody has been charged with it for goodness knows how long. In any case, a private ceremony, however offensive to any of us, cannot be held to have depraved public

10

morality or caused civil strife. I seem to have read somewhere there was a case of blasphemous libel—'

'In 1921,' said O'Brien. 'The chap was convicted and his appeal was dismissed.'

'That's a long time ago, but Uncle Nick tells me there's another prosecution coming up. You know how Halloran always gets all the news. Apparently they considered it too difficult to try to get a conviction for an obscene publication, so they decided on the other. But even the photograph you describe, unless distributed in some way, could hardly qualify for that description. In any case ... look here, what does this chap Letendre want exactly?'

'To get it stopped,' said Jenny. 'That's obvious. And I suppose I should add without causing any scandal, which makes all this talk about the law, however interesting, quite superfluous.'

'That's it exactly!' said Kevin, replying presumably to the first half of her statement. 'But I'm damned if I know how it's going to be done,' he added ruefully.

'Who is the – the celebrant anyway?'

'I forgot to tell you they've a sort of tame chaplain living with them whom they call Father Gowdie, though he's never impressed me as being the genuine article.'

Maitland grinned. 'No odour of sanctity?' he asked.

'If you like to put it that way. I don't know the family except through Georges, though I've dined there a few times when he's been staying.'

'Perhaps you could try some sort of intimidation through him. Would the Johnsons persist, do you think, if he were out of the way?'

'I haven't the faintest idea.'

'Well, let's think about it a minute. If Monsieur Letendre went to him, said he'd consulted a lawyer on the matter, and talked vaguely about outraging the feelings of any Christian by ridiculing or vilifying their beliefs, or by scurrilous, offensive or abusive behaviour, wouldn't that do the trick? If it didn't he could tackle his sister on the same lines, though I have to tell you, Kevin, from what you tell me of the lady it doesn't sound to me as though he'd get very far.'

11

'No, I don't think so either,' said O'Brien gloomily. 'I'll think about it, and talk to Georges again, and if you come up with any better idea for goodness sake let me know.'

'I will. Do you think they're also going in for what might be called a more ordinary type of witchcraft? Laying spells on people and things like that?'

'Do you think they'd work?'

'No, I don't think so. But I wouldn't like to take a bet on anything like that. Saint Thomas said witchcraft is so enduring that it admits of no remedy by human operation.'

'If you mean St Thomas Aquinas, that was a long time ago,' O'Brien pointed out. 'It was certainly believed in once, but I always thought that spells worked because the people at the receiving end believed in them too.'

'In any case it's beside the point. I wish I could help you, Kevin, but it's so far beyond the bounds of reason that it's difficult to apply any ordinary rules. Look up a few good scarifying phrases and see if Monsieur Letendre would like to try a little moral blackmail. If that doesn't help, I can't think of anything that will.'

'Well, I'm grateful to you for listening to me anyway. And I hope I haven't scared you, Jenny. I didn't mean to.'

'Not a bit of it.' Of the three of them Jenny seemed perhaps the least moved, a fact which was explained, to Antony's satisfaction at least, when they were alone together later. 'They must be awfully unhappy to go in for things like that,' she told him, and didn't need to explain who she was thinking of. 'I shall pray for them,' she added. 'After all, if they're worshipping the devil there must be some way of getting round it.'

MICHAELMAS TERM, 1976

'Thank you, I could have worked that out myself. I haven't heard from them yet about Greta's statement, but they know it isn't urgent.'

'No, except that it might go a certain way towards convincing you. Have you spoken to Kevin?'

'Yes, he's writing out a statement for me. Antony, do you really think—'

'I think we might as well go to lunch,' said Maitland firmly. 'It's no good our arguing any more until we have something to go on and there's one point I'll allow you, even at the risk of increasing your scepticism. Can you really see Granville as a member of a coven?'

'I can't see anybody in that light,' said Geoffrey frankly.

'I realise that by this time, but I expect you know Granville, by reputation at least.'

'Bernard does.' (Bernard Stanley was Geoffrey's partner, who dealt with what may be called the more domestic side of their practice.) 'I didn't mention the witchcraft business to him because I can't see it coming to anything, but I did ask whether he knew Granville and he said he did. Dry as dust was how he described him, and you know that for Bernard to say that about anybody—'

Maitland grinned. 'Yes, I see your point. Whatever Georges Letendre may have thought, I think we can rule Jane Granville out of the picture, if only because she'd hardly ever be available. But the people we've heard of as being closely associated with the Johnsons come to a round dozen if you exclude her and her father.'

'I suppose you're implying that that has some significance.'

'Certainly. A coven usually consists of twelve people, in addition to the leader who is often referred to as the devil. So unless one more intimate friend turns up—'

'They must know any number of people besides the ones we've heard about,' said Geoffrey unwillingly.

'Yes, but "intimate" is the operative word. Anyway, who lives may learn. What time is our appointment with the Desmoines?'

'Half past two.'

'Will he be there?'

'Monsieur Desmoines? So I understood. My information is that he is of independent means and has no employment. Come to think of it, you were there when I was told that.'

'The devil finds work for idle hands,' said Antony sententiously, and before Geoffrey could protest that this remark was uncalled for he got up briskly. 'Uncle Nick and I happen to be on speaking terms at the moment,' he said, 'so if you'll promise not to start discussing my perversity with him we may as well go to Astroff's for lunch.'

II

Lunch-time passed peacefully and the subject of Georges Letendre's murder was scrupulously avoided. As they were a little early for their appointment Antony and Geoffrey lingered over their coffee, but they presented themselves at the Desmoines' house a few minutes before the appointed hour. It was smaller than that belonging to the Johnsons, but unless it had come to either of the occupants by inheritance, both it and its rather opulent furnishings conveyed to Maitland that the independent means his friend had spoken of must be ample indeed.

They were admitted by Augustin Desmoines himself, a man in his sixties, tall and thin and a little stooped, with sleek grey hair brushed back from his forehead and immaculate tailoring. Madeleine Desmoines too, as they observed when they followed their host into the drawing room, had the knack of dressing with considerable flair. She was, they decided later, at least ten years younger than her husband, unless it was merely that she had taken more pains to preserve her looks. Antony thought he detected a likeness to her cousin, Françoise Johnson, but she was a much smaller woman, and fair-haired rather than dark. Horton had already introduced himself and his companion, and now Desmoines presented them to his wife with a formality that was perhaps understandable in the circumstances. 'We are sorry to intrude on you at such a time,' Geoffrey assured her.

'*N'importe m'sieur*. If there was any way in which we could help you.' Like her nephew, her English was heavily accented but fluent, and her husband in his turn was to display the same facility. 'But alas, there can be no doubt of what happened. Françoise has told me of all that occurred that dreadful night.'

'Yes, madame, we have already heard her story.' Maitland took over the conversation smoothly. 'Mrs Johnson is your cousin, I believe, but you were not yourself at her house the night Monsieur Letendre died. Or your husband?'

'We were not. So you see—'

'*Doucement, ma mie*,' her husband interrupted. 'These gentlemen know their own business best. You will be seated, *messieurs*, and tell us how we can help you.'

'Thank you.' The two visitors obeyed his gesture, and Desmoines went to sit beside his wife on the sofa, taking her hand in his. 'You understand that we are working for your nephew, Emile Letendre,' Antony went on.

'*Le pauvre*. But you cannot think that he is innocent, *m'sieur*,' Madeleine Desmoines protested.

'To do our best for him,' said Maitland, sidestepping the question neatly, 'it is essential that we know something more of him and of his father. We can't approach Mrs Johnson, because she and her husband will be appearing for the prosecution, and so we come to you.'

'Emile is my cousin, not my nephew,' she corrected him. 'But in view of what has happened, what can we do?' She glanced uncertainly at her husband. 'Murder is a dreadful thing, but to kill one's father! I do not know where he will find forgiveness.'

'Have you lived in England for long?' asked Maitland, dividing the question between them. Better perhaps to come at the subject obliquely.

'Since fifteen years.'

'It seems then that you like our country,' said Antony, smiling.

This time it was Augustin Desmoines who answered. 'It is our home,' he said simply. 'Our friends are here now.' He paused, but seemed to think that this statement needed further amplification. 'And perhaps we should not have come if

Madeleine had not missed her cousin so deeply. They were very close as girls, and after Françoise married an Englishman and came to live here—'

'He means,' said Madame Desmoines, returning Maitland's smile, 'that I have tormented him to come.'

'I'm sure Mrs Johnson was glad of that.' His voice remained deliberately casual.

'I think so,' she told him seriously, as though the matter were of some importance. 'To have someone to share her interests ... we have so many things in common, all four of us.'

'I've read some of Alan Johnson's books. He knows his subject very thoroughly.'

'That too is an interest we share,' Augustin Desmoines put in. 'I think I have been able to – to broaden his horizons a little,' he went on, obviously pleased with the phrase. 'To cover some aspects of French and European history which had not previously interested him.'

'When you were girls together, madame, you and your cousin, I don't suppose such serious matters concerned you.'

'*Ah non*. With Françoise it is always *la bonne aventure*.'

'Foolishness,' said Desmoines quickly. 'But all children seek adventure, do they not?'

'It's very natural. Madame, if you knew Mrs Johnson so well, you must also have known her brother.'

She glanced again at her husband before she replied. 'Georges is older,' she said. 'Five years older than Françoise. 'Now that is nothing, but as children ... he thinks we are silly girls and will have nothing to do with us.'

'But when you grew up?'

'It is strange, but I have seen more of him these last few years than ever before. He was much occupied in Paris with the family business, and after our marriage we lived in Rouen, Augustin and I.'

'But since you have lived in London, did you not see him when he visited his sister?'

'*Certainement*. But until the last five, six years when Emile was in England too his visits were very rare.'

'The branch here has been established for longer than that, has it not?'

'Yes, but usually the manager would go to Paris when it was necessary to consult with Georges.'

'But during these last few years ... I am sorry to press the matter, madame, but as I told you it would help us enormously if you could tell us something of Georges Letendre's relationship with his son.'

Madeleine Desmoines closed her eyes for a moment as though by so doing she shut out some sight that she found unbearable. It was her husband who replied. 'You will understand it is a painful subject for us. Indeed, though, there is nothing we can tell you. Their relationship was a completely normal one, or if anything, from what one could observe, rather more affectionate than is sometimes the case.'

'You saw something of Georges Letendre these last years at least. How would you describe him?'

This time it was Augustin's eyes that sought his wife's. 'You may think perhaps that I should leave this question to you, *ma mie*, since Georges was your cousin. But perhaps I can regard him with greater dispassion.' Madame Desmoines opened her eyes again and made a slight gesture with her hands which evidently he took as an invitation to proceed. 'Georges is, I think I must say, an intolerant man, but naturally this did not disclose itself in his dealings with his friends, or in this case with his sister's friends or with ours. But I've heard him speak sharply to Emile about something concerning the business, and I have always believed he was the type of man to expect unquestioning obedience from his children.'

'I didn't know ... has Emile any brothers and sisters?'

'No, that was merely a manner of speaking.'

'And how did Emile feel about that?'

'When we have seen him alone, here or *chez* Françoise, he has always answered very properly our enquiries about his father. When we have seen them together there was no evidence of anything but a very proper feeling, even, as I have said, of affection.'

'And Emile?'

'Again it is I who must answer you. We have both an affection for him, and you will understand that this is distressing for my wife. Emile – how can I put it? – has been welcome here

65

at any time, and I know that the Johnsons' home too has been open to him. But he is young, he has his own affairs, his own interests. We have seen, I think I must say, less of him than we would have liked. But this – this dreadful thing! Who could have foreseen it?'

'I can understand that it came as a great shock to you both. I believe you dined at the Johnsons' at least once during Monsieur Letendre's recent visit. Was Emile also present on that occasion?'

'No, it is now a month at least – perhaps more – since we have seen him.'

'Then you know nothing of any disagreement between him and his father?'

'Only what Françoise and Alan have told us since the tragedy.' He paused and smiled. 'Is it permitted that I tell you?' he asked.

'Here, in the privacy of your own home, there can be no objection in the world,' Maitland assured him.

'It is Françoise who has told us, there is a strain that last evening between the two of them, Georges and Emile. And she wasn't surprised when her brother asked permission after dinner to talk alone with his son.'

'Had she any idea of the cause of the disagreement?'

'A surmise only. She thought perhaps it concerned Jane Granville. She thought – we had all thought and hoped – that Emile was falling in love with her.'

'Would that have been a cause of dissension?'

'I tell you only what Françoise thought. To Jane there could be no objection, her father is a friend of theirs as well as their *homme de loi*, but she thought perhaps Georges had arranged a match in his own mind for Emile with a French girl, a neighbour. Or perhaps it was merely that he felt Emile had gone too far in the matter without his father's consent. But you must understand that nothing was said openly, this is her idea, no more.'

'Yes, I understand that. Do you know Miss Granville?'

'Yes, certainly. Not so well as we know her father, who is near our own generation, but well enough. A delightful girl, if frighteningly intelligent.'

'That does not make her any the less delightful,' said Madeleine Desmoines, coming back into the conversation with sudden energy. 'You have agreed with me, Augustin, how good it would be to welcome her as Emile's bride. And now – poor child! – what must she be feeling?'

'I gather from what you say that Emile was in love with her. Is that, too, a matter for conjecture, or has he ever told you as much?'

'He has said nothing, but it is of all things the most obvious.' It was clear that she regarded matters of the heart as purely within her province.

'And do I also understand that Miss Granville returned his regard? In your opinion at least.'

'That is more difficult to say. These English girls, they are so self-possessed. But we had hoped—'

'I think, *ma mie*, that now we should pray that Jane's affections were not touched,' Desmoines put in. 'The affair cannot now have a happy outcome.'

'No,' she agreed mournfully, and produced a lace-edged handkerchief to dab at her eyes. 'But this cannot be of help to you, *messieurs*. We are gossiping only.'

'On the contrary, madame,' said Antony, conveying as well as he could that this was a matter of politeness only. 'We wanted to know, Mr Horton and I, whether you could tell us anything of Emile's friends.'

'Only what we have told you already.' Augustin took over again smoothly. 'Jane we know because we know her father, but otherwise it is as I said, Emile had his own affairs.'

'People who knew Georges then, or who might have met them together at the Johnsons' house?'

'Françoise has told us of the friends who were there that evening.'

'Yes, we have their names but cannot approach them either.'

'That is perhaps a pity. We dined there – do you remember the date, Augustin?'

'I believe it was the twenty-eighth of October. A Thursday at any rate.'

'Yes, a Thursday. That was a family party, you understand, except for Father Gowdie.'

'Was Emile present?'

'No, as I said, it was some time since last we saw him, not during George's visit. But Françoise has told us that Bill and Isabel Sampson and Gregory and Lilith Herries had been with them the previous Sunday, and that Keith Thomas had dined with them two days before. But I do not think that any of them could tell you as much of Georges and Emile as we have done, and, myself, I cannot see how it would help you.'

'Don't remind me that we are trying to make bricks without straw. This – Mr Thomas, did you say? Is he known to you?'

'Yes, very well. He is a composer, what they call the soundtrack for films, I believe. But I think – do you not agree, *mon cher*? – that if it were not for the books he writes, he might sometimes go hungry.'

'That is something we cannot possibly know,' said Augustin quietly. 'But I agree, his novels are certainly better known than his music. Romances,' he added with a smile. 'My wife tells me they are very good ones.'

'I see. I think ... unless there is something else you want to ask while we're here, Geoffrey.'

'One thing only,' said Geoffrey, but he came to his feet as his spoke. 'You mentioned Father Gowdie. Is he a Catholic priest?'

'Of course – 'Madeleine began, but again her husband interrupted her smoothly before she could go on.

'A very brilliant man, a Doctor of Divinity,' he said. 'He was ordained in America, I believe.'

'I was thinking that perhaps Emile might have asked his advice, or that Georges Letendre might have confided in him if he was worried about his son.'

'If that had happened he would certainly not have mentioned it,' said Desmoines rather reprovingly.

'One last question then,' said Geoffrey, 'if you will forgive me for pressing the matter. Would you say Emile Letendre was of an impulsive nature?'

There was a pause. Again Madeleine Desmoines consulted her husband with a glance and again it was he who answered. 'Yes, *m'sieur*,' he said, 'I'm afraid I would. Very impulsive indeed.'

III

'Well, that was a load of nothing,' said Geoffrey in disgust when they had made their farewells and were alone in the street outside.

'Do you really think so? As we're so near home we may as well go there for tea,' said Antony.

Geoffrey had no fault to find with this latter suggestion and fell into step beside him. But he would not, as Maitland knew well enough, leave the subject of the recent interview without worrying it as a dog might a bone. 'If you're going to tell me that this Keith Thomas whose name has just been introduced into the matter can take Luke Granville's place as the thirteenth member of the coven, all I can say is you're stretching the matter to suit your own theory.'

'I wasn't going to say anything of the kind,' said Antony mildly. 'All the same, since you suggest it, I think we ought to see him too.'

'If we must,' Geoffrey sounded resigned. 'But if that wasn't what you meant, what was it? Or were you just trying to sound enigmatic?'

'I never try to sound enigmatic.'

'And the name Lilith came up again, but we knew already that's what her friends call Mrs Herries. And I can pass on to Cobbolds that they should look for the Reverend Philip Gowdie in America. If he's really a distinguished scholar that should make matters easy.'

'As for that, we shall see. I have my doubts about him, because I don't think from what Kevin said that Georges Letendre was the sort of man to have the wool pulled over his eyes very easily.'

'An intolerant man, according to our latest information,' said Geoffrey.

'Yes, and his son is impetuous. You walked smack into that one, Geoffrey, don't you know better than to lead a witness?'

'I—'

'Yes, I know, like Uncle Nick you're thinking we should go

69

for diminished responsibility. But I'll forgive you, because it just went to confirm my opinion of our host.'

'What do you mean?'

'Just that he's an extremely clever man. Didn't you notice how he stepped into the breach, usually before his wife could make any incautious remark? But if she did come out with something unwise before he could put his oar in he was all ready to smooth away the rough edges.'

Geoffrey thought about that for a moment. 'You could look at it that way,' he agreed after a while, 'but I just thought Madame Desmoines was a nice woman, genuinely concerned for her young cousin.'

'As for the latter, I'm inclined to agree with you. She won't say anything to contradict the Johnsons' story, as a matter of expediency, but that doesn't mean she wasn't fond of Emile. As for being nice, I'll grant you that too . . . for the moment.'

'Well, you can't say that amounts to a very good afternoon's work.'

'Not if that was the only thing we've learned.'

'What else, for heaven's sake?'

'That Madeleine and Françoise grew up together. 'Didn't you find that illuminating?'

'No,' said Geoffrey baldly.

'Desmoines and Johnson have a common interest in history, perhaps their wives share that too. But when they were young that wasn't what the girls used to talk about.'

'Adventure,' said Geoffrey in a disgusted tone. 'All children like to think of themselves as the heroines or heroes of some favourite story.'

'Yes, that's exactly what I meant. Her husband implanted that idea in our minds very smoothly, or thought he did. But what do you think *la bonne aventure* means?'

'A good adventure, I suppose.'

'Literally, yes. It also means fortune-telling. And I think Desmoines interrupted so quickly because he wasn't at all sure what further indiscretions his wife might indulge in. It's not such a far step from fortune-telling to spiritualism, and that . . . well, it might lead anywhere.'

Geoffrey came to a full stop and turned and stared at his

70

friend. 'You really mean that, don't you?' he said incredulously.

'All I mean is that it's suggestive,' said Antony. 'And don't tell me again that I'm twisting facts to suit my own ideas.' He took Geoffrey's arm and began to urge him onwards. 'I can do with my tea even if you don't want any,' he said. 'And you can use our telephone to make some appointments for tomorrow,' he added, as though this were an added inducement. 'And we may even find Keith Thomas's name in the phone book.'

Jenny was surprised but pleased to see them at that hour and departed immediately for the kitchen, saying over her shoulder, 'The kettle's on already.' So Geoffrey got down to his telephoning immediately, calling his own office first to say he wouldn't be back that evening.

While he was doing that Antony was busy with the phone book, where he found amid the mass of Thomases one with the initial K whose address immediately caught his eye. 'It must be our man,' he told Horton as the solicitor replaced the receiver. 'His address is the same as the Sampsons, only 14A instead of 14.'

'That's convenient, anyway.' Geoffrey had taken out his notebook and was consulting it. 'The Sampsons are the couple who also live in Herriot Square,' he said after a moment. 'I wonder if it's a setup like yours here, the house being divided.'

'It could be, I suppose, but if he's in we'll soon find out.' He shoved the book under his friend's nose, pointing at the same time to the name that interested him. 'Have you got the numbers of the other people?'

'Yes, I have them here.' Geoffrey picked up the receiver, saying as he did so, 'I wonder why the Desmoines consented to see us.'

'Curiosity,' said Antony. 'I can't imagine any other reason for any of that gang being willing to be interviewed.' But Geoffrey was already dialling, and Antony wandered away from the writing table to take up his usual stance near the fire.

In the event the arrangements were made easily. True, Dr Sampson was out, but his wife expected him home by five o'clock most days, and they would both be willing to receive the two lawyers after that hour on the morrow. The K. Thomas

Antony had unearthed proved to be Keith, and the right one. An appointment was made for four o'clock. 'And be sure you press the right bell,' he advised, 'because my landlord lives downstairs and doesn't much care to be disturbed unnecessarily.' After that the Herries agreed to make themselves available at two o'clock. 'That's a good time for me, I just won't go back to my studio after lunch,' said the male voice on the other end of the line.

'No difficulties?' asked Antony as Geoffrey joined him by the fire.

'None at all. It's odd,' said Horton slowly, 'not one of them exhibited the slightest surprise, nobody said, I can't see how we can help you, or anything of the sort. What do you make of that?'

'I should say that Desmoines had been busy at the telephone as soon as we left them,' said Antony. 'It was only to be expected after all.'

'By you perhaps. That presupposes they all have something to hide.'

'I think they do. I know what you're going to say, Geoffrey, even if they are dabbling in the occult it doesn't mean that they had anything to do with the murder. But *if* they're all part of the coven I think they were all present at the Johnsons the night Georges Letendre was killed. It's a slim chance but we may learn something.'

'We may.' Geoffrey's doubt was only too evident. The remark, between two men who had worked together so often, needed no amplification, but in any case he was distracted by Jenny's arrival at that moment with the teatray. He went across to help her, while Antony pulled a table in place to receive it, and to Maitland's relief his friend did not return to the subject again.

But they were not quite done with it that evening. Geoffrey, who had to fetch his car from its parking spot in the city and drive to his home in Wimbledon, where he and Joan had recently moved, was just on the point of leaving when the telephone rang. Antony went across to answer its summons, and was greeted by Gibbs's voice, sounding aggrieved. 'There's a young lady here asking for Mr Horton,' he said.

'He's still here,' said Antony, suppressing the desire to add, As you know perfectly well: because he was pretty sure that at that time of day the old man would not have left his post in the hall. 'Did she give you her name?'

'A Miss Granville. Apparently Mr Horton's office told her that he was here.'

'Ask her to wait a moment, one of us will be down. There you see, Geoffrey, what comes of being conscientious. If you hadn't made that telephone call to the office she wouldn't have been able to track you down.'

'Who on earth—?' said Geoffrey, coming to his feet.

'I think it must be Jane Granville. I'll go down and fetch her, shall I? Vera may be in the study, and anyway Jenny's presence will ease the strain for her if there is any.'

'Yes, of course. I'm sorry, Jenny,' Geoffrey was saying as the other man went out. 'She must have been very insistent, or my people would never have sent her on here. They're pretty discreet on the whole.'

'It doesn't matter,' said Jenny. 'I realise it must be tiresome for you to be tracked down like this, but I'm quite used to it. I'll just take out the tray, but I think it's late enough to offer her a drink if any refreshment is called for.'

'Let me,' Geoffrey offered. So they were both in the hall on their way back from the kitchen when Antony and the unexpected visitor arrived.

'It is Miss Jane Granville,' he told them. 'And you've already made your apologies,' he added, turning to the girl, 'so there's no need to repeat them. This is my wife, Jenny, and the man you're looking for, Geoffrey Horton.'

Jane Granville, as they learned later, was twenty, but she looked younger. A fair girl, rather pale, but with a face that came very near to real beauty. She acknowledged the introductions with a smile. 'All the same I think I should apologise to you, Mrs Maitland, and to Mr Horton too. I'm afraid I bullied his secretary into telling me where he was, but Mr Maitland has explained the position to me, that he's Emile's counsel, so perhaps it's all for the best. From my point of view at least.'

'Of course it is. Come in and sit down,' said Jenny warmly. Her family and friends would have said that it was her habit to like everyone on sight, but – as she told her husband later – in this instance she felt especially drawn to the newcomer. It might have been sympathy, of course, but she didn't think so.

As soon as they were seated Geoffrey took over. 'Well now, Miss Granville, what can I do for you? Mr Maitland, I gather, has told you that we both wanted to see you, though we thought it would have to wait till the Christmas vacation. But before you say anything I ought to tell you that your father refused to talk to us, because he felt his professional connection with Mr and Mrs Johnson made it improper for him to do so.'

'That's just like my father. He told me how he felt, but of course it doesn't apply to me,' Jane protested. 'And I know it must seem strange to you, but I only heard last night what had happened.'

'How was that?'

'I hardly ever look at a newspaper when I'm studying but Emile usually telephones me every few days, and when the weekend passed without his doing so I tried to ring him and got no reply, so I phoned home instead. I was absolutely furious when Father told me, because he hadn't let me know. It was too late then to get a train, but I came up this morning.' She turned to smile at Jenny. 'I spent the afternoon cross-examining Father,' she said, 'but he really doesn't know anything except what he learned when he attended the Magistrates' Court with Mr and Mrs Johnson. So then I thought the proper thing would be to see Mr Horton, and perhaps he could tell me—' she broke off there and when she spoke again her remarks were addressed to the two men indiscriminately. 'I hope you understand, it's quite dreadful not knowing. I know Father wouldn't lie to me, but I can't believe in what he says happened.'

'If he told you that Emile Letendre, who is our client, had been arrested for the murder of his father, I'm very much afraid it was quite true,' said Geoffrey. 'If you're a friend of Emile's I realise this must have come as a shock to you.'

'A friend? We were going to be married!'

Watching her Maitland realised that her self-possession, which at first he had wondered about, was very hard held. A kind word, he thought, was all that was needed to wreck it, and nothing could be less helpful at this point than tears. 'What else did Mr Granville tell you?' he asked in a deliberately noncommittal tone.

She turned quickly to face him. 'Not just that,' she said, 'but that there was no doubt at all that he was guilty. I don't believe, I won't believe that's true.'

He smiled at her ruefully. 'You're putting us into a very awkward position, Miss Granville. It's early days yet, Mr Horton has had no papers from the prosecution, nor has he had the opportunity to decide what line the defence should take. If your father attended the Magistrates' Court hearing he knows almost as much as we do.'

'He said Mr and Mrs Johnson's evidence would prove conclusively ... and that there were four other witnesses to confirm their story. They're his aunt and uncle, I like them so much, I didn't think they'd say a thing like that about Emile.'

'I'm afraid you must face the fact—'

'That they accuse Emile ... yes, I accept that, I have to. But that he hurt his father, never!' She looked helplessly from one of them to the other. 'You're his lawyers, surely you believe him.'

'Whether we do or not makes no difference to the strength of the prosecution's case,' Maitland told her gently. 'I think myself that we shall find there's a good deal to be said for the defence, but its preparation is not far enough advanced as yet for me to say that positively.'

'Are you trying to tell me he did it but there may be some extenuating circumstances?'

'That wasn't what was in my mind, but let's think about it for a moment. Did you know Georges Letendre?'

'I've known him for years ... well, since I was fourteen or fifteen. Father always dined with the Johnsons when he was visiting them, and as soon as I was old enough they used to ask me too. But Emile loved his father, I know that, and I loved him too, he was such a – such a good man. That sounds silly – doesn't it? – but it's the only way I can think of describing all his qualities. He was kind, and I admired him because he'd always stand up for what he felt was right, not in an aggressive way but quietly and firmly, even if his point of view was an unpopular one.'

'Can you give me an idea of the sort of things you have in mind?'

'Oh, things that I've heard Emile call faith and morals. He was a Catholic, you know, as Emile is, and Emile never tried to persuade me but I've been taking instruction. And I have to admit that it was knowing Monsieur Lentendre that made me decide, all on my own, to do that. Father says they quarrelled. Was that true?'

'Emile has told us that it is.'

'But did he tell you – ? Father says Mrs Johnson thinks it was about me.'

'I'm afraid neither Mr Horton nor I can answer that question, even to you, Miss Granville. But if it was true, how deeply do you think Emile might have resented it?'

'He isn't a child and this isn't the Dark Ages. He could marry who he liked.'

'Forgive me, that doesn't quite answer my question.'

'Well, of course—' There was a pause while she thought that out. 'He'd have been angry, but he'd have been grieved as well. He wouldn't have liked going against his father, but he wouldn't have changed his mind, I'm sure of that. Or . . . Mrs Maitland, am I being sentimental?'

Jenny smiled at her. 'If you are, it's in a very pleasant way,' she said. 'But, you know, I don't think you're the sort of person to have been misled about a thing like that.'

'I was afraid you might think I was being awfully stupid.'

'We've been told,' said Antony, reclaiming her attention, 'that Emile is impulsive.'

'Who said that?'

In his turn Antony smiled at her but shook his head. 'Is it true?' he insisted.

'Again there was a pause while she considered the question. 'I suppose it is,' she admitted. 'He isn't old enough yet to have learned to be cautious.'

'He can still give you quite a few years.'

'Yes, I know. Do you think that could be what Monsieur Letendre objected to? If Mrs Johnson's right about that, I mean.'

'If he knew you half as well as we're beginning to, even on

such a short acquaintance,' said Maitland, 'he must have realised that you're a very wise young lady. And don't think I'm being patronising when I say that, I mean it very sincerely.'

For the first time her cheeks acquired some colour. 'We weren't going to be married until I got my degree,' she confided. 'Father had set his heart on that, and though I don't care about it one way or the other I didn't want to annoy him unnecessarily.'

'How did Mr Granville feel about your engagement?'

'We weren't properly engaged because of meaning to wait. But he knew about it, of course, and I think he was glad because he liked Emile. Only now he says I'm obviously well rid of him.'

'I hope you don't feel that too,' said Antony, and encountered an admonishing look from Geoffrey, who recognised as well as he did that he had come perilously near to telling her his real opinion.

'No, because ... it's a dreadful thing to say but I think whatever he'd done I'd still feel the same way about him. Are you trying to say that if they quarrelled about me and Emile lost his head it might make things better for him?'

This time Maitland yielded to impulse. 'I think I may tell you that that course has been suggested to our client, but he refused it. He told us he wouldn't admit to a lie.'

'That's all right then; of course, it's all right, Mr Maitland. If he says he didn't do it, he didn't.'

'I'm glad to have your assurance on that point, of course,' said Antony. Jenny gave him a quick look, suspecting sarcasm, but saw at once that he was perfectly serious. 'I think, love,' he added, turning to her, 'we could all do with a drink. Would you mind seeing to it?'

Jenny got up immediately. 'Is sherry all right for you, Miss Granville?'

'Yes, but—'

'But what?' asked Geoffrey when she hesitated.

'I can quite see that you're not going to tell me anything, and I realise now I shouldn't have expected you to. So I don't see what else there is to talk about.'

'On the contrary,' said Geoffrey, managing to sound

77

avuncular, 'we've told you – or rather Mr Maitland has – as much as we know ourselves, and perhaps a little bit more.'

'I know you have to be discreet. I shouldn't have come,' she said, for the first time not trying to hide her distress.

'You're wrong about that, we very much wanted to see you,' Horton assured her. 'Will you tell us how long you've known Emile, and when you decided to get married?'

She gave him a doubtful look, as though she suspected that the question had some hidden meaning. 'Ever since he came to England,' she said. 'I only used to see him at the Johnsons, of course, but then about a year ago we began to get more friendly. When I was home last summer we saw a lot of each other, but it wasn't until I was just going back to Oxford – well, the weekend before – that we really started making plans. That's when I told Father, and once he knew we were willing to wait he was as pleased as could be. But now I wish we hadn't put it off, because I don't suppose—'

Jenny had come back quietly, and now placed a glass at her elbow. 'You'll feel better when you've drunk that,' she said. 'And I really don't think you should worry yourself into being ill, because that won't help Emile when he comes home again. He has to face the grief of his father's death, you know.'

'But will he come home?' Her tone pleaded for reassurance and Jenny's heart – always, according to Antony, as soft as butter – melted.

'I wish I could honestly tell you I was sure he would,' she said. 'But I can assure you that my husband and Mr Horton are both very experienced in this kind of thing, and you can be certain they'll do everything that can be done.'

'I know that.' Suddenly her smile, encompassing each of them in turn, was radiant. 'They've both been so kind answering my stupid questions, and I've got a feeling . . . but I shouldn't say that, it's just more stupidity.'

'No, don't say it,' said Jenny. 'It really isn't necessary, you know. Because if you want to help, just answer their questions and don't worry too much about what they mean. Antony would say he's fishing in the dark, because at this stage nobody can know what will turn out to be useful.'

'Thank you,' said Jane. She sat back in her chair again and

when Jenny had finished her errand of mercy picked up her glass. Jenny eyed her anxiously while she tasted its contents.

'I hope it isn't too dry,' she said. 'I ought to have thought, there's some Dubonnet if you'd rather.'

'No, this is fine. And you're quite right, it does make me feel better.' Which, considering the small amount she had drunk so far, could only be a downright lie. 'What else do you want to know?' she asked.

It was Maitland who again took up the questioning. 'Anything you can tell us about the people Georges Letendre knew in this country. I gather that the Johnsons and your father had some friends in common.'

'You're thinking someone else might have had a motive for killing him. But could anyone else have got into the house after Emile left him?'

'It seems unlikely, but it's something we have to find out. And you're quite right, it would be more sensible to stick to the people more directly concerned. What about the Johnsons?'

'I liked them both,' said Jane, probably not realising that he laid some stress on the past tense. 'I've always thought there's something a little regal about Mrs Johnson, but she's always been very nice to me. He's different, very quiet, and sometimes seems as if he isn't listening to what's going on. I've read some of his books and he's certainly very clever so I expect he's always got lots to think about.'

'I suppose you didn't see Georges on his recent visit?'

'No, I didn't come home during the time he was here. If you're going to ask me how he got on with his sister, I think he found Mr Johnson easier to talk to. Not that they didn't seem very fond of each other, but I sometimes wondered—'

'What did you wonder, Miss Granville?' Maitland prompted her when she broke off.

'They didn't seem at all like brother and sister. I shouldn't say that as I'm an only child, but that's how it seemed to me.'

'I see. And what about Father Gowdie?'

'I've met him, of course. He lives with them,' said Jane. Her tone was reserved.

'You weren't thinking of going to him for those instructions you spoke of?'

79

talking together, and after the first ten minutes or so no one left the drawing room except your host, Mr Alan Johnson, who was absent for—'

'Two minutes, no more.'

'And at some time after that you heard—'

'A door open and shut rather violently, and quick footsteps crossing the hall. Then the unmistakable sound of the front door being tugged open and slammed shut a moment later.'

'My lord,' said Halloran, 'it is of some importance that the court be allowed to hear exactly what happened from this point on, including any comments made between the witnesses. May I ask your indulgence in this matter if, in some instances, the rules concerning hearsay evidence, are contravened?'

'Mr Maitland?'

'I'm sure your lorship is aware that I would not for all the world inconvenience my friend,' Counsel for the Defence told him dulcetly.

'You see, Mr Halloran? Nobody wishes to compromise your efforts to give the court a clear account of the events of that tragic evening.'

'I am obliged to your lordship. Will you tell us then, Colonel Fielding, what the effect of this somewhat turbulent exit was upon the six people assembled in the drawing room?'

'Françoise exclaimed something that sounded angry, and Alan said, trying to make light of the subject, "It doesn't look as though we'll see Emile again this evening." The rest of us – it was a family row, after all – started talking about anything that came into our heads, but when we heard the hall clock strike eleven Françoise said, "It doesn't seem as if we shall see Georges either, I'm afraid he must have been too upset to rejoin us, but he never goes to bed later than this." And that was all until Cynthia and I were ready to leave at a little past midnight, and of course we offered to see Agnes home. We all went out into the hall – Philip is more of a friend to the Johnsons than Alan's secretary – and Alan said something like, "They left the light on in the study", and when we looked the door was closed but you could see the light quite clearly shining underneath it. Alan went across to turn it off and a moment later cried out in horror. Of course we all hurried to join him.

Georges was lying on the hearth-rug with the poker not far from his head. I'm not unfamiliar with death, and was able to ascertain that he was beyond all human aid without in any way disarranging things. Françoise was deeply upset, but as soon as she had composed herself we sent for the police.'

'Thank you, Colonel, that's very clear. Now, to forestall a question I'm sure my friend is waiting to ask you, in your opinion would it have been possible for any unauthorised person to enter the house from the time you heard Emile Letendre leave it and the time you discovered his father's body?'

'I'm able to assure you that it would have been quite impossible. Alan suggested immediately that we three men should look around the house. First we ascertained that all the outer doors were locked. The front had a Yale latch, which had locked itself when Emile slammed the door behind him, the kitchen door was locked and bolted on the inside. Then we examined the windows – they too had not been tampered with – and searched the house, but I'm afraid by this time it was more as a matter of form rather than anything else. It was only too obvious what had happened.'

'Yes, Colonel Fielding.' For once in his life Halloran spoke rather hastily. 'That is for the jury to decide. Now I have only to thank you for your cooperation, and turn you over to my friend Mr Maitland. I'm afraid he will have some questions for you.'

'Indeed I have.' Counsel for the Defence was on his feet in an instant. 'I'm afraid we must go back to the evening of the thirty-first of October last, Colonel Fielding. Do I understand that, with the exception of Georges and Emile Letendre, all the party gathered together at the Johnsons' house that evening were familiar friends?'

'That is so.'

'Of some years' standing perhaps?'

'Ten years at least, I should say. We met the Johnsons first through Madeleine and Augustin Desmoines. Madeleine and Françoise are cousins.'

'And gradually the rest of the party were added to your circle of . . . friends?'

'Actually we're only talking about Agnes Ripley.'

160

'So we are.' Maitland's assumption of surprise could not have been more convincing. 'I was becoming confused, I'm afraid. Mr and Mrs Johnson seem to have had such a large circle of intimate friends.' He paused a moment, but the witness did not attempt to make any comment on this as he went on, 'You would not then consider the Reverend Philip Gowdie as among their number?'

'Indeed I should, but we were speaking of long-standing friendships, I believe. I have only known Philip since he joined their household about three years ago.'

'As secretary to Alan Johnson?'

'Yes. I believe his duties mainly concerned research.'

'Did Mr Johnson previously have help of this kind with his work?'

'No. That is . . . not, I think, except for occasional typing. But I expect . . . I'm sure the need for assistance grew with his popularity.'

'As a writer?'

'That's what I meant.'

'Now, Colonel Fielding, you have told us that you are rather vague on the subject of time so I won't question you further on that point, which my friend has already covered. But one thing puzzles me a little. We know for certain that Mr Johnson's call was received at the police station at precisely twelve-thirty, and yet you say that the body of the deceased was discovered a little after midnight. Can you account for the delay?'

'In the circumstances I think it was very understandable. Françoise was his sister, you know.'

'I haven't forgotten that.'

'She was upset. The women were with her, and the rest of us searched the house as I've already said, to make quite certain that no intruder was present. Or could have obtained access.'

'Unless he was provided with a key, of course.' (Was that enough – he hoped it was enough – to create the impression that this was his line of defence?)

'The police officer told us later that Georges's latchkey was in his pocket.'

'There was nothing to stop him, however, having one cut.' Counsel seemed for the moment to be speaking to himself.

161

'You have mentioned noticing a sense of strain between the two Letendres at dinner that evening. How did this manifest itself?'

'Emile was very quiet and hardly addressed his father.'

'Was that unusual?'

'From the few occasions I had seen them together previously, yes.'

'When you heard – how did you put it? – a door open and close, followed by footsteps in the hall, that might have been the door to any of the rooms leading off the hall, might it not?'

'Yes, I suppose so.'

'Yet you immediately reached the conclusion that it was my client leaving Mr Johnson's study?'

'It was obvious, wasn't it? There was no one else in the house.'

'Did it not occur to you that Emile Letendre might have left a little earlier, after which another visitor arrived?'

'We should all have heard that.'

'Not, for instance, if Georges Letendre had let his son out and admitted the other visitor at the same time. That could have happened, couldn't it?'

'There would scarcely have been time. Alan Johnson was quite positive it was Georges's and Emile's voices he heard from the study, quarrelling, and that was certainly not more than ten minutes before Emile banged out of the house.'

'You've said yourself, Colonel Fielding, that you're inclined to be vague about time,' said Maitland, but he sounded thoughtful and the words were hardly a question. 'Because of that I feel bound to put this one last query to you ... are you completely sure that Mr Johnson left the drawing room to fetch the cognac before the visitor – my client, or whoever it may have been – left the house in so noisy a fashion?'

For the first time the witness's face was scarlet. 'You're saying ... you're implying—'

'I'm implying nothing, Colonel Fielding. I asked you a simple question, and I should be obliged if you would give me a simple reply.'

'Very well then, of course I'm sure! He came back to the drawing room at least ten minutes before we heard Emile leave.'

Halloran re-examined briefly, apparently in an attempt to soothe ruffled feathers before the witness was allowed to step down. In this, to Maitland's surprise, he was completely successful, his attitude – we're two simple men and we know a fact when we see one – going down extremely well with the witness. After a few moments he was directed to a seat in the body of the court and his place was taken by his wife.

Cynthia Fielding was a very tall, fair woman who had surely come straight from the hands of her hairdresser. This was, of course, as Maitland knew, quite impossible but the effect was there just the same. She wasn't a raving beauty but her features were regular and her complexion flawless and she was dressed attractively but with extreme propriety. 'What the well-dressed witness was wearing,' said Derek Stringer in his leader's ear, but Maitland's attention was already lost to anything but the woman in the witness box.

She took the oath clearly and with a sort of reverence that immediately caught Antony's attention. Unless he was very much mistaken this was a clever woman, and it might be to his advantage not to antagonise her by frivolous objections during Halloran's examination-in-chief.

So far as facts went, her evidence echoed nearly enough that given by her husband, though she claimed a closer friendship with Françoise Johnson, as perhaps might be expected. 'Alan has his work,' she said, 'and is conscientious about it besides. In those circumstances, a wife can sometimes be lonely and in need of companionship from her womenfriends.'

This time Bruce Halloran had lowered his voice to its most sympathetic pitch. 'This is very understandable. She must also have missed her family in France.'

'As to that there was only Georges, once Emile came to live in England.' She paused to look sadly at the accused and wiped away an invisible tear before she went on. 'And with Georges, there was much affection, you know, but they had very little in common. But to have him taken from her, and in such a way . . . it passes belief, it passes almost what can be borne.'

'Yes, indeed,' said Halloran, but Maitland thought, with a touch of cynicism, that he looked very much like a man who, having sown the wind, has no desire to reap the whirlwind.

'And on the night of the thirty-first of October—' Counsel for the Prosecution added, giving her a nudge in the direction he wanted her to go.

'Ah, yes, I'm straying from the subject. You must forgive me, this is all so very distressing.' Except in the matter of time, to which she seemed to have given extraordinary attention, her evidence coincided with her husband's. Emile had arrived late, but his aunt had told him to hurry with his drink and they had gone into the dining-room precisely at eight thirty, leaving again at ten fifteen. It had been obvious that Emile was ill at ease with his father, something about the business, she had thought at the time, and nobody had been surprised when Françoise had packed them off together to the study to have their talk while the rest of them went to the drawing room. Again she was quite clear about times. Alan Johnson had been absent from them for no more than two or three minutes, his errand evidently not having necessitated a visit to the cellar. She would put the time around ten forty, and it had been ten minutes later exactly when Emile left the house. She knew nothing, of course, of the search the men had made, but knew a good deal of Françoise's sufferings and the lengths to which she and Agnes had had to go to console her. Here for the first occasion her sense of timing seemed to desert her but she assured Halloran earnestly that they had all been completely occupied, it would in no way have been possible to put in a call to the police earlier than they did.

Maitland opened his cross-examination cautiously. He didn't think she was the type of woman to indulge in hysterics, but he wouldn't put it past her to pretend to do so, and he didn't want any headlines of that kind to greet Uncle Nick when he opened his favourite newspaper tomorrow morning. 'You're obviously a very good friend of Mrs Johnson,' he said, 'at a time when she most needs her friends.'

'We have been *sympathique*, as she herself would say, since first we met,' she told him, looking at him with curiosity. Not even his nearest and dearest would have applied to Antony the adjective 'handsome', so often used by the newspapers to describe his uncle, but he was a pleasant-looking man and for the moment seemed to have her approval.

164

'That must be a comfort to her now, and to her husband too. The other lady who was there that evening, Mrs Catherine Ripley—'

'Agnes Ripley,' she corrected him quickly.

'You must forgive me. Is she also an old friend?'

'Yes, and lonely too, since her husband died two years ago.'

'You were, in fact, a close-knit group? The Johnsons are fond of entertaining, aren't they?'

'Oh yes, we see a lot of them, and of their other friends.'

Maitland cast a quick look at his opponent and saw the beginning of a frown forming on Halloran's face. He went on in a hurry, 'Concerning Georges Letendre—?'

'Well, he is a friend of mine perhaps more than of my husband.' she smiled at him confidentially. 'His business, you see, is of great interest to a woman. We have all visited their plant in the country and have all received samples, too, and I, like Françoise, would use no other kind of cosmetics.'

'Which could need no greater recommendation,' said Maitland, wondering how far he could go in this line. 'So you knew Georges and Emile Letendre perhaps a little better than Colonel Fielding did.'

'Yes, I think that's true.'

'And that evening – All Hallows Eve, was it not? – you say that my client seemed ill at ease with his father. Will you go into a little greater detail for us, explain exactly what you mean?'

'It isn't easy.'

'That I realise only too well.'

'Well, I will try. Alan had gone to let him in, and when he reached the drawing room he greeted his aunt first, of course, and then the rest of us in the rather punctilious way he had, and then instead of joining Georges, as would have been natural, he went and sat beside Agnes Ripley. I don't even think, if I must be honest with you, that he likes her very much. I thought it was just to avoid conversation with his father.'

'I see. Was there any discussion between them then about talking alone after dinner?'

'No. I got the impression later that Georges had already arranged all that with Françoise.'

'Well, I dare say he'd spent the whole day with his father at the office, and there was nobody present of his own generation, so perhaps his choice of a companion was not so strange after all. In any case, you say it was only a few minutes before you went in to dinner.'

'Yes, that's true. But if any of us had realised—'

'Come now, Mrs Fielding, you mustn't say anything to anticipate the jury's verdict.' Maitland's tone was still indulgent.

'No, of course not, but it's obvious . . . after all, we all know what happened.

Counsel for the Defence caught the judge's eye. He had no desire himself to check the lady's indiscretions, but fortunately his lordship took the hint.

'Precisely, Mr Maitland,' said Mr Justice Carruthers. 'Mr Halloran, you really must prevent your witness from making these unwarranted assumptions.'

And there was the fire that she had been keeping damped down so successfully. 'Unwarranted, my lord?' She whirled on the judge. And then, catching a rather stony look, she drooped again. 'I'm truly sorry, your lordship, but to see such dear friends suffer—' The handkerchief was brought delicately into play again.

'We can all understand how painful it must be to a lady of your sensibility,' said Maitland, thinking as he spoke that if ever he'd seen a witness who was as tough as an old boot, this was it. 'In his evidence, your husband referred to the Reverend Philip Gowdie, or Dr Gowdie as I believe I should call him, as being Mr Alan Johnson's secretary. From what I have heard, the position seems rather an odd one for him to hold.'

'Not at all!' For the first time her answer to him came a little sharply. 'It was I who suggested the arrangement to Alan, he was working far too hard, and to have someone to help in the research work was just what he needed. Dr Gowdie had been forced to retire from his – er – his ministerial duties because of ill-health, but I feel it was a good arrangement that has benefited them both.'

'Yes, I'm sure you can congratulate yourself on a good deed well done. We seem to have covered everything, Mrs Fielding, so unless my learned friend wishes to re-examine—'

166

But Halloran didn't, so she was allowed to join her husband and her place was taken by the witness who interested Maitland perhaps more than all the others put together – the Reverend Philip Gowdie, who, from being referred to as the Johnsons' chaplain, had now suddenly become Alan's secretary, or research assistant.

Dr Gowdie turned out to be a tall, thin man who reminded Maitland irresistibly of an Old Testament prophet. Even Halloran seemed a little taken aback, but he recovered himself quickly once the oath had been taken and elicited details of the witness's name, his Doctorate of Divinity from an American university, and his present position as nominally retired but helping his kind host in whatever ways he could.

It soon became evident that here was one witness whom no judge, however severe, would have a hope of keeping in order. He assumed at once that the trial was a mere formality, a preliminary – really unnecessary – to Emile's conviction.

However, so far as his confirmation of the evidence already given was concerned, Halloran at least could have had no complaint. He was precise as to the events of the evening, including the time schedule, and described the search for any possible intruder, or for any means of ingress into the house, in all the detail anyone could have wanted. During the period he had lived with the Johnsons in Herriot Square, Georges Letendre had visited on an average of twice a year, but they had little in common and he couldn't claim a friendship with the man. As for the younger Letendre, he had a mind of his own and though he was always polite and respectful to his aunt and uncle, it was quite obvious that he would suffer no interference with his own affairs. That went for his father too, and Maitland's objection at this point was not well received. Halloran, however, seemed to derive no consolation from this, and had the air of one relieved of an almost intolerable burden when at last he was able to hand over his witness to his learned friend for cross-examination.

At this point the judge intervened, adjourning the court until the following morning. It was later than any of them had realised, so Maitland, after a brief word with his colleagues, thrust the majority of his books and papers into Willett's hands,

167

saying that he would go straight home. He had often had occasion to thank heaven for Willett, who had adopted his interests years ago and had his own ways of circumventing old Mr Mallory when it seemed expedient to do so. This evening he received his burden cheerfully, and Antony decided that on the whole a taxi would be a good idea.

III

When he let himself into the house in Kempenfeldt Square he saw immediately, to his relief, that the study door was closed. This emotion was tempered a little, however, by Gibbs, who came forward from his favourite lurking place at the back of the hall to say, 'Sir Nicholas asked me to tell you, Mr Maitland, that he and Lady Harding would take the liberty of calling upon you this evening after dinner, if that is convenient to you.' The politeness of this message, which led Antony to believe it had been delivered almost word for word, left him speechless for the moment, but he recovered in time to ask the butler in the most flowery phrases he could call to mind to convey his compliments to his aunt and uncle and inform them that he and Mrs Maitland would be entirely at their disposal at the time mentioned. Having done this he took himself up the stairs to his own quarters, where Jenny, seeing at once from the stiff way he held himself that he was more tired than usual, refrained from questioning him about the day's events, though she was obviously so full of questions that after a moment he burst out laughing.

'Uncle Nick and Vera are coming up after dinner,' he told her, 'I suppose they must be curious too. Can you wait till then?'

'I suppose I must,' said Jenny with mock indignation, and no further mention was made of Emile Letendre and his affairs till the party from downstairs came at about nine o'clock. Roger had also arrived by that time and Antony was only too glad to turn over to him the task of providing the newcomers with suitable refreshment.

For once Maitland, in spite of his restlessness, had gone back

168

to his chair after greeting Vera ... 'The only time,' as Sir Nicholas had once told him sourly, 'that you treat your aunt with the proper respect.' This was probably true, but they were far too good friends by now for any formality to persist. Now Maitland looked across at his uncle and said with a flicker of amusement in his tone, 'And what report have you received from the battlefield, Uncle Nick?'

'Nothing much. You've embarked on entirely the wrong line of defence, which Halloran, with what he knows, or perhaps I should say doesn't know, was bound to conclude; and as he thinks it's too late now for you to change your line, he didn't feel there was much harm in saying so. But I must say I'm anxious to hear your side of it, what you've tried to achieve and how far you think you've succeeded.'

'And you've got past the official witnesses and reached the really interesting ones,' said Vera. 'I want to know your opinion of them, and I'm sure Jenny does too.'

'Yes, she was patient enough to wait so that I'd only have to tell the story once. I was trying to get over the impression that our argument would be that Emile had left the house earlier than the witnesses believe, and that in seeing him out Georges admitted another visitor who returned to the study with him and caused his death. It was this second man they heard leaving the house and slamming the front door behind him. I think actually I succeeded pretty well, though there were some questions I had to ask the pathologist that didn't really fit that theory. However, if Halloran just believes I was trying to be awkward or clutching at straws or something like that, there's no harm done. The questions I asked about the fingerprints on the poker wouldn't have spoiled my effect.'

'Do you really think it may not have been the murder weapon?' asked Vera.

'Yes, I really do. I have a sort of picture that keeps repeating itself in my mind like a roll of film, but I'm not going to bring Uncle Nick's wrath down on my head by telling you about it, it's far too vague, and admittedly pure guesswork.'

Roger had finished his task by this time and resumed his own seat. 'When Vera referred to the interesting witnesses,' he said, 'I presume she meant the people who were present at the

Johnsons that night besides the Letendres.'

'Yes, and she was quite right, they were a study in themselves. I'd formed a mental picture of Colonel Fielding – he's retired, by the way – which of course proved to be completely wrong. He's by no means typical, though occasionally I got the impression that he was trying to play the part. For instance, he made a point of saying he wasn't very given to noticing things about other people, and then he volunteered the information that Emile and his father had been on strained terms that evening. Also he was vague about time ... the bluff soldier, you know the kind of thing.'

'It might have been true,' said Jenny thoughtfully.

'So it might, love, if he hadn't been quite wide-awake enough to give me all the correct answers that would tend to incriminate Emile. He was followed by his wife, Cynthia, a very exquisite lady who really needs a whole page of description to herself. She was quite clear about exactly what had happened that evening, and when, and about the fact that Emile arrived late and seemed to be avoiding his father, she thought at the time because of some business disagreement. Incidentally, the slight delay in calling the police was explained by the fact that she and Agnes Ripley had their hands full in trying to comfort Mrs Johnson, while the three men of the party were searching the house, and making sure that there was no way anyone could have got in or out. I shall try for some confirmation of that point ... I'm quite sure they're right, but the jury may as well hear it well-rubbed-in from their own lips.'

'All this must have taken some time.'

'Yes, it did. There was just time for Halloran's examination-in-chief of the next witness, who happened to be Dr Gowdie. The story now is that, being retired for reasons of ill-health, he's doing some research work for Alan Johnson. Both the previous witnesses mentioned that as well. His factual story coincided with theirs exactly, which was only to be expected. That's about all, I think, except that when cross-examining Mrs Fielding, I slipped in just one reference to All Hallows Eve, instead of giving the date as we'd all been doing before. She didn't turn a hair ... well, I hadn't expected her to start like a guilty thing surprised, or anything of the sort, so I wasn't disappointed. All I can hope is that it may give the group of them something to chew on this evening. I'll venture a little further tomorrow, it may do some good and it may not but at least no one else will suspect what I'm getting at at this stage and a weekend's reflection may help matters along.'

Sir Nicholas, already lying back at ease in his chair, had closed his eyes in pain about halfway through this speech. 'I think perhaps that is all we can any of us bear tonight, my dear boy,' he said now, raising his cognac to his lips with a deliberately unsteady hand. 'If you have induced a mood of concentration in the enemies' ranks, why not say so? The phrase you used is a singularly revolting one.'

FRIDAY,
the third day of the trial
I

When Maitland rose to cross-examine Philip Gowdie the following morning, the witness's look of having strayed from the pages of the Old Testament was still foremost in his mind. Though why a gaunt look and somewhat unkempt appearance should provoke such a comparison, he couldn't decide. Halloran had already reminded the witness of the continuing efficacy of his oath, and repeated a few of yesterday's questions. Now, as Gowdie turned to face Counsel for the Defence, Antony became aware of a sort of malevolence that emanated from the man. No word had yet passed between them yet the antagonism was there, unmistakable and as obvious as if it had been spoken aloud.

He schooled his voice to an easy, conversational tone. 'Perhaps you will forgive me, Dr Gowdie, for beginning with a question that is not strictly relevant. Were you born in the United States of America or is the slight accent I detect a result of having lived there for many years?'

'I am American born but I can no longer claim citizenship. England has been my home for many years and I have taken out naturalisation papers. As you may know, under those circumstances an American loses his own citizenship.'

'This is a pity, but I'm glad you liked our country enough to wish to stay here. Your own home state—' He raised his hand as Gowdie seemed about to speak. 'No, let me see if my guess is correct. You come from Louisiana?'

'Originally, yes. You know that part of the country?' (Halloran was looking definitely puzzled, but there was nothing after all to which he could object, though there was always the possibility that his lordship might grow tired of this exchange.)

'No, I've never been so far south. But I have a friend in New

172

England and I recognise the accent from having spoken with friends of his from the same part of the country. Your – your alma mater, the college from which you received your doctorate, is further west, I believe.'

If he had flattered himself that Gowdie was relaxing, that last remark put a stop to it. 'That is quite correct,' said the witness cautiously.

'Yes, I have the record somewhere. Ah, here it is.' He held a large sheet of paper between his hands and gazed down at it admiringly. 'This is a photocopy, you understand. What I believe is referred to as a mail order degree, Dr Gowdie.'

'If you wish to belittle my poor endeavours.' (Maitland, with obvious insincerity, muttered something of a disclamatory nature.) 'There are times when the work to be done in the saving of souls must come before the self-indulgence of allowing oneself a conventional course of study.'

'Yes, of course, I should have thought of that. You're a minister of religion then?'

'Certainly I am.'

'I do not wish to pry too closely into so intimate a matter, but may I clarify one point? Are you a member of the Church of Rome?'

'I am not!'

Maitland almost yielded to the temptation to remark, sotto voce, 'Four hundred religions and only one sauce,' but he managed to restrain himself, saying instead, 'I asked that question only to clarify a matter that has been puzzling me. Mrs Johnson's brother, Georges Letendre, was certainly a Catholic, as is my client, and I heard that she referred to you occasionally as her chaplain. Now it seems that your position in the household was of a different nature.'

'If you knew Mrs Johnson you would also know that she is kindness itself. My position, as you call it, might be regarded as somewhat anomalous; to put it frankly, I'm glad to have a roof over my head and only too willing to help Mr Johnson as far as I can in his research. Perhaps she feels I find this degrading, I don't know. But as she and her husband are both practising Catholics it is certainly very far from the truth that my living in their house has anything to do with religion.'

'I see, a family joke. And now we've heard your story of the

173

night of Georges Letendre's death, and it is obvious that you are a man of some perception. During the three years you have lived with the Johnsons you have had some opportunity of observing both my client and his father. Will you tell us your impressions of them?'

'That isn't easy. I can't say that I'm well-acquainted with either of them.'

'An impression at least,' said Maitland coaxingly. 'Georges Letendre, for instance. Living in the house, you must have seen a good deal of him whenever he visited his sister.'

'Not as much as you might imagine. During the day he was, I suppose, at his place of business, and even when he was at home at Herriot Square my own duties would keep me occupied. You will understand, I am sure, that work in the historical field is not always easy to lay aside at a moment's notice. I find it interesting, and quite often continue reading in my own room purely for pleasure.'

'I can quite see that would be so, but still there must have been occasions when you were in Monsieur Letendre's company. One of the previous witnesses referred to him as a simple, friendly man. Would you agree with that estimation?'

'Far from it!' The witness seemed, to Maitland's eyes, to grow at least a foot as he spoke. Here was the Old Testament prophet back with a vengeance. 'He was intolerant, a bigot, hostile to anybody whose beliefs were different from his own.' (Shades of the scarlet woman.)

'Surely you didn't discuss religion at the dinner table,' said counsel innocently.

'That was not what I meant. His whole attitude ... I assure you, I was not mistaken.'

'I see. My client then, Monsieur Emile Letendre.'

'You ask me that, and he a parricide?'

'Dr Gowdie.' That was Mr Justice Carruthers intervening without waiting for Maitland's appeal. 'You say you have lived for many years in this country, so I'm sure I don't need to explain that Monsieur Letendre, though he stands accused of murder is regarded as innocent until his guilt is proved. That remark was extremely improper and will be stricken from the record.'

Halloran was on his feet again making some sort of apology; the judge picked up his pen again with the air of one well-satisfied with what he had accomplished; Maitland turned back to the witness, who seemed to have grown at least another six inches. 'I am much obliged to your lordship,' he said, but his eyes were on Gowdie, as he spoke. 'As the matter is already imprinted in the jury's mind, however, perhaps you will permit me one question in clarification.'

'That will be quite in order, Mr Maitland.'

'I'm obliged to your lordship,' said counsel again. 'Tell me, Dr Gowdie, did you mean to imply by your rather indiscreet remark a moment ago that you had known for some time that Emile Letendre intended to kill his father?'

'Certainly not! Only looking at the matter afterwards—'

'Ah yes, with hindsight. That can account for a good many of the troubles in this world, Dr Gowdie, as a man of your experience must know. But tell us what you thought of my client before you jumped to the conclusion that he had killed his father.'

'The conclusion was not one that could be escaped,' said the witness, and this time Halloran was on his feet before the judge could speak.

'I must apologise, my lord, but at the same time I should like to point out that my learned friend in some sense invited that comment.'

Mr Justice Carruthers inclined his head. 'You may be right, Mr Halloran, but you really must keep your witness in better order. That remark, too, will not appear in the record, Mr Maitland—'

'My lord?'

'If you could refrain from – from teasing the witness, perhaps your cross-examination of him would continue more quickly.'

'If your lordship pleases. I should like Dr Gowdie, however, to answer my question as to his opinion of my client before the events with which this trial concerns itself.'

'Certainly, Mr Maitland, that will be quite in order. Dr Gowdie?' he added enquiringly.

'As far as I could tell he was a well-behaved young man,' said the witness grudgingly, 'very courteous to his elders and particularly to his aunt and uncle, Mr and Mrs Johnson. I did, however, from remarks he made from time to time, come to the conclusion that he was a self-willed young man, and on the night of which we are speaking it was perfectly obvious that he had quarrelled with his father at some time quite recently.'

'Did you also decide what the quarrel had been about?'

'I can only give you a conjecture. Business matters perhaps, or perhaps Monsieur Letendre objected to the kind of life his son was living now that he was away from home.'

'What kind of life was that?'

'I have no idea. It was merely a thought that came to me.'

'I see. Now you spoke a moment ago about Monsieur Letendre's intolerance towards people of a different faith to his. To what ministry were you ordained?' This was delicate ground, and even Derek, who so rarely argued about matters of policy, had protested when he mentioned his intention of raising the question.

'I am a member of the Ancient Order of Levellers.' (The witness was now at least eight feet high, or so Maitland told his family that evening.)

'I came across a co-religionist of yours some years ago in the north of England, but I didn't know the order existed in the United States.'

'Yes indeed. Our membership there is much larger than it is in this country. In fact, in the south of England I have found no opportunity of attending a service.' He had relaxed a little and now he looked deliberately around the court before he spoke again. 'But all this, I'm sure, can have no relevance to the conduct of your case.'

'Yes, Mr Maitland,' said Carruthers, looking up. 'Dr Gowdie has anticipated a question of my own. What is the relevance of all this?'

'In one sense it has no relevance at all, my lord, but I'm laying the foundation for two questions that I'm very anxious to ask this witness.'

'Two questions?'

'I believe so, my lord.'

The judge looked at him hard for a moment, glanced at Halloran, who of course made no sign, being content enough to abortionists, and, as it turned out, they were combining these activities with acting as conveyors of the means . . . to get rid of an unwanted husband, for instance. The first evidence was obtained by the use of an *agent provocateur*, and by the date I have mentioned the secret court, which permitted of no appeal from its judgements, was brought into being. At this time a number of other fortune-tellers came under investigation, notably one Catherine Monvoisin, commonly known as La Voisin. The fortune-tellers, as I should have said, in addition to the activities I've already mentioned, sold love philtres where required.'

'Resourceful ladies, it would seem.'

'Yes indeed, but I'm straying from the subject. As the investigations went on, increasing evidence was found that the Black Mass had been celebrated not once but on many occasions. Some of the noblest in the land were involved and it became evident that Madame de Montespan was not only at the very heart of the satanism but was also using her connections with La Voisin to attempt to poison the King. She had been for many years his mistress, but now he had turned to a younger woman. I dare say she turned to witchcraft first when his affections cooled, before resorting to more desperate measures, but that is at best a conjecture. At this stage, the noblest in the land being involved, it became necessary to find a means of suppressing the scandal. No doubt some innocent people suffered, no doubt many escaped through the suppression of evidence at the insistence of the King. These included the Marquise de Montespan, who was eventually allowed to retire to a convent with a large pension.'

'I wonder what Reverend Mother thought about that,' said Maitland, forgetting himself again for a moment. 'Now, Professor, you have given us some very helpful background information. I wonder if you can tell us something about the practice of witchcraft today.'

'There is no doubt at all that, in one form or another, it has become extremely active again. On all levels, that is to say from the lady who offers to read your tea leaves, to the covens we have mentioned, the black magic and to satanism. Of the less harmful forms – less harmful because they hurt nobody but their practitioners – people will speak openly. There is, I understand, no law to prevent them.'

'Only the Fraudulent Mediums Act, and I challenge even my learned friend Mr Halloran to get a conviction under that one.'

'Yes, yes, of course, but where more serious matters are concerned—'

'Luckily we needn't worry about that. Let's get back to the Black Mass. Is that still being performed today?'

'Without a doubt of it. But it is naturally not spoken of so openly by its adherents. It is not so long since in this country—'

'You are referring to Alastair Crowley?'

'Yes, and before him to the Hellfire Club. Though my own opinion is that their activities were mainly of a pornographic and – ah – wanton nature.'

Maitland for a moment was distracted by the use of the word, so rare nowadays, but he couldn't afford to let his attention wander. 'And now?' he asked.

'In highly sophisticated circles, in cosmopolitan communities in the great centres . . . New York, Paris and here in London.'

'My friend will certainly ask you, have you proof of this?'

'I can offer no proof,' said the professor regretfully, 'but I can assure you that it is something I know of my own knowledge, as you lawyers say.'

'Your lordship, may I ask that the witness be shown the piece of paper which I entered as an exhibit, on which Mr O'Brien copied down what was written on the torn sheet that Georges Letendre showed him?'

'Certainly, Mr Maitland. I'm sure if he can enlighten us about those names we shall all be grateful.'

The usher obliged, and Professor Goodheart studied the paper for a moment. 'Perhaps you will be kind enough to read it aloud to us, Professor,' Maitland urged.

'Certainly. "*By Adonai, by Prerai, by Tetragrammaton, by Anexhexeton,*" he paused, looking up. 'It breaks off there, but if I may guess at the ending, "*by Inessesensatoal, by Pathumaton, and by Itemon!*"' declaimed the professor.

'That sounds most impressive,' said Maitland when he had finished. 'Are you able to tell us its meaning?'

'Certainly, it must be familiar to any student of the subject. It is part of a demoniac conjuration and can be found in Lemegeton, a medieval grimoire.'

'Thank you, Professor,' said Maitland again. 'I hope that satisfies your lordship's curiosity,' he couldn't resist adding, turning to the judge.

'To a certain extent, Mr Maitland, to a certain extent. Have you any more questions for this witness?'

'No, my lord. Anything further would be repetitious, and I don't want to delay my learned friend any longer.'

'Very well, Mr Maitland. I'm sure we are all obliged to the witness for a very instructive discourse,' Carruthers concluded. 'Mr Halloran?'

But Counsel for the Defence had been wrong about his opponent's intentions. His learned friend had thought up a much more subtle way of rendering the professor's discourse valueless. 'I have no questions for this witness, my lord,' he said as Maitland sat down. 'With all due respect to your lordship I cannot help but feel that this evidence is irrelevant and of no concern to the case.'

At this point, mercifully, Carruthers decided to take an early luncheon recess. That gave them a little more time than usual and they made for Astroff's where they had the table to themselves. Whether Sir Nicholas's conference was still in full swing, or whether he was perhaps lunching with his instructing solicitor, Antony didn't know; but on the whole he was grateful at the moment for his uncle's absence.

Geoffrey was practically gibbering. 'Now what do we do?' he said. 'I was relying on Halloran to keep him for the rest of the afternoon.'

'You've got Madeleine and Augustin Desmoines up your sleeve,' Antony pointed out. 'Trot them out, Madeleine first I think, and I'll spin out my examination of them as long as I can. Then with any luck we'll get to Lilith bright and early in the morning.'

'Do you really think that's so important?' asked Stringer. 'With all that's been said on the subject I doubt if they'll be holding their revels tonight.'

'You may be right about that, but I'm counting on Athenais's influence. I'd say she was the leading spirit, wouldn't you?'

'Probably but—'

'The others are in it ... oh, for any one of a thousand reasons. Boredom probably. But she, if I mistake not, is a true believer. It's pretty certain they use drugs, most of them perhaps at no other time, but Lilith was certainly under the influence when we saw her, as you'll admit, Geoffrey. I'm just hoping that whatever she takes at the ceremony won't have worn off by morning, or that she'll have given herself a bit extra for luck.'

'It seems awfully chancy,' said Derek doubtfully.

'Of course it's chancy! It's our only hope, Derek, and I'll admit it's a damned small one, but don't let's give up hope until it's all over.'

'Anything you say,' said Stringer equably, and for the moment the subject was dropped.

II

Maitland arrived home that evening to find, as so often happened, that Sir Nicholas had returned before him and had already taken Vera up to join Jenny. When Antony went into the living room he found his uncle cross-examining his hostess as to the precise nature of their dinner, which she had incautiously referred to as a 'fish thing'. Nobody can remember a recipe, it would have been no use in any case as he knew well enough; not that Jenny was secretive, but because she made dishes up as she went along. Now she got up with some relief to greet her husband. 'I'll pour you a drink, Antony. Why don't you sit down?'

That came perilously close to telling him he looked tired, and that nagging pain in his shoulder was more obvious than usual. He looked down at her for a moment, and then smiled. 'A good idea, love,' he said, and went across to take the chair opposite his uncle's. 'Good evening, Vera. Hello, Uncle Nick. Have you been here long? I came straight from court and thought for once I'd be ahead of you.'

232

'After an extremely boring luncheon,' said Sir Nicholas, 'I awarded myself a free afternoon.'

'Pity you couldn't do the same thing,' said Vera, more gruffly even than usual, as was generally the case when something had happened to touch her feelings. 'Look as though you've had a bad day.' She knew by now that this came only too near to the forbidden subject, but she wasn't above disregarding the custom that had grown up among the other members of the family when she considered it appropriate.

Maitland met her eyes and his smile was rueful. 'Thank you, love,' he said, as Jenny put down the glass at his elbow. Then, 'I've had better, Vera,' he admitted.

'No need to talk until you feel like it.'

'Thank you, Vera, but this is something that needs airing and I'd rather get it over with. You know, of course, all of you, the aspect of Halloran's examination of Kevin O'Brien yesterday that we all so scrupulously avoided mentioning last night?'

His eyes were on his wife as he spoke and she nodded vigorously. 'Even I could work that one out,' she said.

'Well, the whole beastly business jumped out and hit me before I got across the square this morning. Godalming was waiting for me at the corner of Avery street. I won't go into the details of our conversation—'

'I suppose you lost your temper,' said Sir Nicholas.

'—but he told me quite clearly that he believed I had recounted Kevin's story to Emile and coached him in the evidence he was to give. He also said something like, "When your client's found guilty there's not a soul who won't believe the same thing."'

'No proof,' said Vera, 'Can't be.'

'I don't think that will be necessary. I'm not saying anyone who knows me would believe it – at least I hope not – but if the story was going around, that would be enough to make the situation very difficult.'

'A miracle of understatement,' said Sir Nicholas. He had abandoned his lounging position and was sitting up very straight in his chair. And then, eyeing his nephew keenly. 'There's more than that, isn't there?'

'Quite a lot more. When I got to court, I was met with a

message that Carruthers wanted to see me in his chambers. Halloran was there too. As a matter of fact' – he smiled a little wryly – 'I was quite sorry for him. He was charging ahead asking all the obvious questions – as I pointed out to him, it was exactly what he should have been doing – and the answer to that one jumped up and hit almost as violently as it did me. What the judge said was that the idea was already current in police circles, which he'd heard in some devious way. I'm pretty sure it was the Johnsons who communicated with Godalming, and the whole thing is pretty irregular, but there's nothing much we can do about that.'

'Had Carruthers anything useful to suggest?'

'He wanted to know if I'd asked your advice, and I told him I hadn't because we both knew I'd no choice but to go on. I think he just wanted to reassure me, as Halloran did, that he didn't believe I'd behaved improperly in any way. Which was comforting, I suppose, but not really helpful. So we all went back to court and got on with things.'

'You'd be calling Professor Goodheart this morning, I believe.'

'Yes, Uncle Nick, and I needn't tell you about his evidence because you've read his book yourself. He appreciated the need for brevity and condensed what he had to say as far as was possible, altogether a brilliant performance. And Halloran took the wind out of my sails completely – after all, as he told me, he still believes Emile is guilty and it's his duty to prove it if he can. What he did was get up and say he has no interest in cross-examining this witness, the evidence he had given was completely irrelevent to the case.'

'Yes, I see. You were rather hoping he'd spend the whole afternoon over it, weren't you?'

'I was. I don't know whether the Johnsons will hold one of their usual parties or not tonight, but I'm counting heavily on their doing so. Professor Goodheart is pretty sure that their sessions are more drug- and sex-oriented than anything else. Sorry, Vera.' (Vera, had been at the Bar herself until her marriage, gave one of her grim smiles at this unnecessary piece of thoughtfulness.) 'When we saw Lilith before she was obviously drugged, but whether she's hooked on them or whether she'd given herself a shot – or whatever it is they do – to keep her spirits up for the interview, I don't know. But there's at least a chance she may turn up in court in talkative mood, and another chance – don't bother pointing out how slim it is, Uncle Nick – that I'll be able to get something useful out of her.'

If Maitland had needed any confirmation that his uncle was worried, it was evident in the fact that Sir Nicholas had so far refrained from complaint about his occasional mangling of the English language. 'I'm not quite sure from what you say whether this Mrs Herries has appeared in the witness box yet or not.'

'No, Geoffrey had the Desmoines standing by, she's Emile's cousin, you know, though pretty much the same age as Mrs Johnson. I examined them both as though I'd called them as character witnesses, having despaired of confusing the jury by introducing the witchcraft thing. It was extremely tedious, and I suppose really funny if I'd been in the mood to feel amused. It was still a little early when Halloran finished with Augustin Desmoines, and I actually re-examined until I was sure Carruthers would think it was time to adjourn. So we still have that one small vestige of hope left to us. If Lilith breaks down and admits that there was some funny business going on, even if she goes no further than that it would scotch the rumours. But it might not help Emile, and he needs help badly,' he added, looking round at each of his listeners in turn. 'He's not taking prison life easy. Do you remember Jon Kellaway? He had a touch of claustrophobia too, which I think is what's wrong with Emile, and a long sentence will be sheer hell for him.'

There was a brief silence after that. Jenny was remembering the years – all too many of them – when the sound of a key turning in a lock had been sheer agony for her husband, and even sitting in a room with the door closed had required an effort of will on his part. She said after a while, because the silence was becoming unbearable, 'Geoffrey is looking after things tonight, isn't he?'

Antony smiled, for the first time that evening with genuine amusement. 'He certainly is,' he confirmed. 'He's as conscious as we are, of course, of the unpleasant possibilities, so he told me at lunchtime that he's having Cobbolds put five men on the job – and damn the expense – which, supposing they turn up, would allow everyone we expect to be shadowed home. Agnes Ripley is the only one who isn't a couple, but Keith Thomas lives in the same house as the Sampsons, so that should cover everybody. Not that it would be the slightest use unless Lilith says anything and we could use it as confirmatory evidence. And that's too much to hope for, I'm afraid.'

'If your description of your conversation with the lady when you and Geoffrey visited her is anything to go by,' said Sir Nicholas, 'I imagine there is no cause for despair yet. So I suggest we let the subject drop until later in the evening, when we might go over your examination of her in more detail. I should like to know how you propose to set about it, and – one never knows – I may have a suggestion or two to make myself.'

Antony picked up his glass which so far had stood beside him untouched. After he had sipped a little of the straw-coloured liquid he managed another smile. 'That's a good idea, Uncle Nick. It's some time now since we discussed the matter in detail, and things were quite different then.'

So it was quite late when his uncle and Vera finally left. Jenny piled the coffeecups and glasses on to a tray but did not attempt to take it out to the kitchen. 'Vera and I weren't really talking much while you and Uncle Nick was discussing Lilith's possible evidence,' she said. 'I think it sounds quite hopeful. After all, you know already that she's rather unstable.'

Antony picked up his glass which so far had stood beside her without attempting to help, now held out his left hand invitingly. 'The last time we discussed the possibility of my having to give up practising law,' he said as she joined him, 'you suggested that it might be a good idea if I became a company secretary.'

'Yes, but Uncle Nick said you'd find that dull. Anyway, Antony, there's no question of your having to give up. As Vera said, there's no proof – how could there be? – and you admit that no one who knows you would believe it for an instant.'

'It isn't so much a question of my giving up, love, as of the law – of it retreating beyond my grasp.'

'All because of a rumour?' said Jenny indignantly.

236

'All because of a rumour,' he agreed soberly. Then he bent to kiss her and his arm tightened about her shoulders. 'My dear and only love,' he said, 'when we're together like this, I find it quite impossible to worry about anything. So long as we're together.'

There was some truth in that, Jenny thought, but certainly not the whole truth. Still, she returned his kiss enthusiastically and spoke no more of the future that night.

WEDNESDAY,
the sixth day of the trial

A brief glance around the courtroom next morning assured Maitland that all the people who had been present at the Johnsons' house on the night of the murder were there, in the seats reserved for those who had already given their evidence. This morning they included Agnes Ripley, the first time she had attended since her collapse the week before. Certainly she looked fully recovered, in fact in quite a bloom of health. The others maintained a grave air of impassivity, but he thought he detected in Françoise – or should he use the name she obviously preferred, Athenais? – a faint air of . . . excitement wasn't quite the word, but a suggestion that she had been through an uplifting experience. He looked from her to Dr Gowdie, as being the most likely person to have shared this emotion, but what could one tell from a face so effectively camouflaged by hair? In any case – he dismissed the idea impatiently – it was certainly no more than wishful thinking.

Beyond an exchange of greetings neither Geoffrey nor Derek made any attempt to engage him in conversation, except that Geoffrey told him briefly, 'They were all in attendance at the Johnsons' last night, as you hoped, and there's a list on your desk of the names of Cobbolds' men who can attest to the fact.'

'Please, God, we shall need them,' said Antony fervently. But by this time the court was assembled, and the judge had taken his place. Maitland got to his feet, therefore, and called his first witness: Mrs Lilian Herries.

The pause that followed seemed to lengthen itself to an almost agonising degree, then one of the court attendants came in, in a hurry, and made his way to counsels' table. 'Mr Maitland,' he said in a low voice, inaudible except to his

238